Scorching Siberian Winter

Zophia R. Kotala

CONTENTS

PART ONE: UNDER THE HOT SUN

Emiliea shivered as a cool breeze swept through her home. It was a welcome change from the 90-degree temperature that normally plagued the winter months of Siberia. She wrapped her shawl around her shoulders as another wisp of wind pushed her long brown hair off her shoulders and flying in the air. She knew she should've put her hair up this morning, but it was always such a pain to brush it out. Not to mention the fact that within minutes the humidity would ruin any hair-do she attempted anyway. It didn't matter now though. With the wind outside, if she went into town, she had to put it up. There was too much of a risk otherwise. With an annoyed sigh, she turned around going back through the drawer of her vanity in search of a rubber band.

"Are you going out today, sis?" Came a voice from behind her. She knew who it was before she even turned around. Kevin was leaning on the doorway, his white hair was a mess of fluff atop his head and his soft brown eyes, so unlike her bold violet ones, shone behind the thick lenses of his prescription glasses.

"Yes," Emiliea responded, returning to gaze at her reflection in the mirror. She picked up the brush in front of her and began pulling it through her tangled curls. "Mom said she needs milk. The fridge broke again yesterday so the stuff we had before spoiled."

"Can I come with you?" he asked eagerly. Emiliea inwardly winced. She knew that all Kevin wanted to do was go outside and explore, but after the outbreak they couldn't risk that. His diagnosis made him more vulnerable to the infection and neither her nor their mother were comfortable letting him be exposed to the airborne illness. That's why they took so many precautions.

"Kev…" she began hesitantly. She didn't want to keep him locked up, but everyone who has contracted it died. Even though the doctors had been able to keep some of them alive for months, there were those who died within days. Those with a preexisting condition usually had only a day or two at most before the disease took hold and Death enticed them away from the land of the living.

"I know," her brother interrupted before she could continue. "I can't risk being exposed." The small boy hung his head low his entire posture radiating disappointment.

"I'm sorry," Emiliea responded quietly. "I wish there was something I could do to help you, but…"

She couldn't finish the sentence and she didn't need to. He may have only been nine, but he had a maturity level greater than most of the adults in the town. They both knew that the disease was the main priority for healers. Every hour of their day and every resource at their disposal was devoted to finding a cure. Any other ailment one may have was not a priority and could go untreated so long as it wasn't contagious. And as far as they could tell from the records left by the Old World Leukemia wasn't caused by a pathogen, but by some other force of nature.

"It's ok," Kevin reassured her, his smile brightening the whole room, even though it wasn't entirely genuine. "Just make sure to say hi to Luke for me," he added.

"I will," she said, pulling her hair back into a high bun and covering it with a headwrap. The cloth would keep out any possible particles which contained the virus so that it couldn't be returned to the house. Grabbing her S-mask she fastened the straps around her ears and adjusted the white filter to cover her face. "I'll be back tonight. Tell mom not to wait for me to start dinner."

"Will do," he replied with an overabundance of cheerfulness before leaving the room with a bounce in his step. Emiliea smiled as she watched him skip away. She missed the ability to be that happy and cheerful. So carefree about everything in the world. She stood there for a few minutes as if trying to bask in her brother's exuberance before she closed the door where he came from and sanitized the room. The process ended in three minutes allowing the front door to swing open so she could step outside into the harsh heat of the winter sun.

She wished, not for the first time, that she could cool down with thinner clothing instead of the long sleeves she wore now. It would be so much easier to cool off if she didn't have so many layers of clothes trapping the heat against her lanky body. With the sunlight beating down rudely and sweat creeping down her neck, it was easy to see why her dreams were filled with crisp cool water and thin tank tops and shorts; bathing suits being the only covering needed to protect against the harsh rays of light.

Fantasizing about that was not something unique to her. In fact, she was pretty sure most people around here dreamed of that every once in a while. She could remember once reading about places in the Old World where that was common. The people would dress in thin clothes and enjoy the feeling of cool clean water on their skin. Such behavior was frowned on now of course. Perhaps if the people of the Old World had been working to solve the issues they themselves had created instead of leisurely strolling on beaches which now lay underwater, the population of the human race wouldn't have been reduced to a fraction of what it once was.

She'd heard stories of the Old World. Apparently, life had never been better for humans. In some places there had even been large councils of people who made decisions for the betterment of their nation. They ruled their lands because the ones who lived there decided they could. It sounded perfect. But she couldn't understand how civilizations of the past had allowed such horrible things to come to pass. If it had been all that great, wouldn't they have prevented the melting? Wouldn't they have prevented the outbreak? Her old teachers said that it was because of the population size and the lack of education of the people. Her mother said it was because they were all corrupt, only wanting money and power and not what was good for the majority. Honestly, she didn't care why it happened. She only cared that it did.

In the distance, a large sand dune came into view, marking the entrance to the town. Emiliea let out a breath of relief as she reached it. She entered carefully making sure that she avoided making contact with the people of the street. They were most often the first infected ones which was why coming in from the outskirts was so risky. Multiple times she'd questioned why her mother didn't move them downtown, near the doctors and healers. But her mom had dodged the question each time never giving a full answer.

She walked another couple of blocks before the Center came into view. The large building towered over the street people's huts and shacks. Its steel grey exterior giving off a cold and distant feeling. Taking out her entrance card, she scanned it at the door and walked in breathing in a sigh of relief when she saw Luke behind the counter at his father's store.

"Hey," She said when she approached

grabbing an apple out of his hand and taking a bite. "How are you doing?"

"I was fine before you walked in," Luke responded with a chuckle taking the apple back and taking a bite of his own. "What brings you by, Emi?"

"What I need an excuse to see my best friend?" Emiliea asked, raising her hand to her chest in mock offense. "You wound me."

"Mhmm, you only ever come into the store when you want something," He shot back leaning forward with a smirk. Emiliea smiled in return before reaching over the counter and grabbing his lunch box.

"Come on," she said walking away while he shook his head in amusement. "I'm hungry and I haven't seen the rest of the gang in weeks. Get someone else to cover your shift for today. It'll be fun."

Luke rolled his eyes before grabbing his walkie from his belt.

"Dad, I'm leaving to hang with Emi.

I'll be back later," he said into the small machine before throwing it down on the counter and coming to stand next to his longtime friend. "There, I told my dad. God, I'm gonna get in so much trouble for this."

"I'm worth it though," Emiliea said shoving his shoulder good-naturedly.

"Yeah I guess you are," he responded, adjusting his mask before they continued further into the Center. "Did you already call Cora and Conner?"

"Nope," she said. Luke gave her an exasperated look before she continued. "It's not a big deal. They'll probably be down by the VR room like usual."

"Yeah, probably," he agreed. "But if they aren't?"

"Then I guess we can hang out just the two of us. I'm not terrible company, am I?" Emiliea asked playfully.

"Ehh. I suppose you're a better conversation starter than Jesse," Luke joked, referring to the cactus he kept in his room. Emiliea snorted in laughter trying not to draw the attention of the crowd.

"The day I'm less talkative than a plant is one I hope neither of us ever see," she replied smoothly.

"Hopefully not," Luke concurred.

They walked a while in silence passing by a couple of shops before they finally arrived at the arcade. The game room was practically empty, with most of the children being locked up at home, or at school. Looking around, Emiliea was struck by how much Kevin would enjoy a place like this. He loved playing the board games she would bring home and when she was busy, he'd usually wind up playing solitaire in his room. It was fun for him, but not nearly as fun as the Old World video games left over from the retro-digital era. Pac-Man, Galaga, Air Hockey… all the things Kevin would probably never get to experience. Her thoughts were interrupted when someone began shaking her shoulders. She turned around to meet Luke's worried eyes as they stared into hers.

"Are you ok?" he asked worriedly. "You kind of zoned out there for a second."

"I'm fine," Emiliea said, her voice shaking slightly.

"Were you thinking about Kev?" he asked knowingly. She nodded slowly not trusting her voice at the moment. How did he always seem to know what was going on with her? She looked up when she felt his large arms wrap around her small frame. "He's going to be ok Emi," he said warmly. "The outbreak can't last forever and once they find the cure, they're going to make sure he gets better. He is one of the strongest kids I know. He will beat this."

Emiliea didn't respond but she moved her arms to hug him back. They stayed in the embrace for a few moments trying to forget the world around them. Both of them yearning for the days of their childhood when they could play outside together and ignore the way everyone and everything around them began to die. After a minute, Emiliea pulled back blinking back the tears that were desperately trying to claw their way out.

"I'm ok," she said firmly, keeping her voice steady. "Let's just find Cora and Conner. I miss us all hanging out together."

"Yeah me too," Luke agreed knowing his friend wanted to change the conversation. "I mean the last time we saw them was back when you still had bangs."

Emiliea winced squinting her eyes. "Ugh no. Do not bring up that dark time in my life. Honestly, I'm not sure why I ever thought that was a good idea."

"I thought you looked nice," Luke said honestly.

"Yes, but you always think I look nice," Emiliea responded cheekily. "It's one of your more charming characteristics."

"I think you'd look better if you let your hair down every once in a while," He said looking over her headwrap.

"You know Angela doesn't want me risking the contamination," she said, like a rehearsed response to the question.

"I know," Luke said with a sigh. "But it would be great."

"You just want me to stop listening to my mother," she shot back, narrowing her eyes.

"Guilty," Luke said with a hearty laugh before continuing ahead, Emiliea following closely behind. "You know I still think it's weird that you refer to your mom by her first name."

"Well, I think it's weird you still talk to your dad at all," Emiliea noted. Luke looked away at the statement shifting from foot to foot.

"Look, I know he's not the nicest guy in the world…"

"Luke, he's a drunk asshole who scares you to death," Emiliea argued. "I just don't understand. You know Angela would love it if you lived with us. She practically thinks of you as a son anyway."

"I don't want to talk about it," Luke sighed, putting his hands in his pocket.

"Fine, I'll drop it," Emiliea said, shaking her head.

They reached the VR room in the back and could hear yelling through the thick metal doors. Both friends looked over, not really wanting to enter in the middle of one of the pair's many arguments.

"After you," Luke said holding his arm out with a smug look. "After all, what was that saying from the Old World? Ladies first?"

Emiliea rolled her eyes moving past Luke and putting her hand on the door handle.

"You're such a baby sometimes," She said with a sigh. Luke shrugged and gave her a nervous glance causing her to smile. Just as she was about to pull open the door, a large crash started from inside. Both their eyes widened as Emiliea threw open the entrance. Cora was holding up her goggles with a look of fury in her eyes holding them above her head. Conner was on the floor below with an arm over his head.

"What the hell is going on in here?" Emiliea asked, looking between the twins. Cora immediately dropped the goggles on the table behind her as Conner leapt up to his feet without a thought.

"Oh, heyyyy Emi," Cora responded, putting her hands behind her back. "What's up?"

"Not much. Just wondering why you were standing over your brother looking like you wanted to kill him," Emiliea responded, shifting her glance over to the other Twin.

"Well it's kind of a long story," Conner said scratching the back of his head.

"No, it's not," Cora argued. "This idiot deleted all my high scores from the game," she explained gesturing to the score screen behind them.

"I did not!" Conner yelled in frustration.

"Then where did they go, huh?" Cora responded, her face turning red.

Emiliea shook her head, unable to believe the way her friends were acting. She knew that they were three years younger than her, but this was ridiculous. They were almost adults. How could they still be acting like they were Kevin's age?

"Maybe they just restarted the system like they did for the game room in the Center for the next town over," Luke suggested. "They deleted everything from when I visited while I was still there."

"See, no reason to kill each other," Emiliea agreed, trying to keep the slight amusement she felt out of her voice. Cora rolled her eyes, a smile appearing on her youthful face.

"I wasn't actually going to kill him,"

she said looking over to her brother.

"Yeah she needs me. How else is she going to stay alive? She's helpless without her big brother," Conner agreed, smirking before Cora slapped him in the arm.

"First of all, you don't know that you're the older one, Mom and Dad never told us that before they passed. Secondly, I'm not the one who accidentally locked themselves in the bathroom when they were younger so if either of us is helpless it's you," she replied crossing her arms in front of her chest.

Conner's cheeks flushed red at the statement as he turned to Cora with an embarrassed look on his face.

"You promised you wouldn't mention that again," he mumbled quietly.

"Hate to tell you this, Con, but everyone in the center remembers you doing that," Luke mentioned chortling slightly. Conner seemed to pale at the statement looking Luke in the eye nervously.

"You are joking, right?"

Emiliea snorted. "Conner even I remember that," she added.

Conner groaned in response running a hand through his short red hair. Cora, Emiliea, and Luke all began laughing at his expense.

"So, Emi, other than helping my sister and friend embarrass me, what brings you by?" Conner asked, trying to change the topic of conversation.

"Why is everyone asking me that?" Emiliea asked shooting Luke a questioning look.

"Maybe because we haven't actually seen you in months," Cora suggested. "Where have you been?"

"Angela has been keeping me locked up," Emiliea responded jumping down onto a nearby bean bag chair. "Kev started coughing a few weeks ago. She was convinced it was because I brought some bug home from the Center, so for the last few weeks I've been forbidden from leaving the house."

"Oof," Conner said, sitting down next to her. "That sucks."

"Yeah your mom seems to be a little overkill on this stuff don't you think?" Cora agreed.

"What do you want me to say? I might be 18 but she still pretty much controls my life," Emiliea pointed out.

"Well, I guess we should make the best out of the time you have left before Mother Gothel locks you up again," Luke said, shoving her to the side slightly to sit down next to her.

"Why are you comparing my mother to an Old World movie villain?" Emiliea asked, turning to look at him. "She may be overprotective, but she's not evil."

"Whatever you say Rapunzel," Cora said giggling. Emiliea rolled her eyes before joining in on the laughter.

"So, what do you guys want to do while her highness is out of her tower?" Conner questioned.

"Well I don't know about you guys

but I'm starving. Someone," Luke said narrowing his eyes at Emiliea, "ate my apple."

"To be fair, you hadn't eaten it yet. It was just sitting there on the counter begging for someone to consume it quickly," Emiliea responded dramatically lifting a hand to her chest. "I saved the apple."

"You stole my lunch," Luke corrected. Emiliea rolled her eyes playfully.

"Yeah. I guess I did. It was delicious by the way," she added with a smirk.

"Well since everyone seems to be hungry, why don't we go and get a bite to eat at the food court?" Cora suggested.

"I never said I was hungry," Conner protested looking at his sister with an annoyed expression.

"You didn't have to Con, I know you. You're always hungry," Cora explained.

"Hey!"

"What? Are you going to try and deny

that?"

Conner pouted for a minute crossing his arms.

"No," he finally ground out. "Why am I always the victim of ridicule in this group?" he asked rhetorically.

"Because you're the easiest target," Luke explained standing up and wrapping an arm around the younger boy's shoulders. "Now come on, let's go get something to eat."

"Luke, you're not one to talk," Emiliea said laughing as she and Cora walked out behind the bickering boys. "You are pretty easy to pick on too.

"Yeah well it's never fair when you and Cora gang up on us," Luke grumbled.

"Oh, come on we're not that bad," Cora replied humorously.

"Plus, it's not our fault that you boys are such easy targets," Emiliea added.

"Yeah I'm going to have to remember that next time you can't figure out that a door is opened by pulling on it and not pushing," Luke said.

"I swear to god that was one time and since then you have never let it go," Emiliea laughed.

"And I never will." Emiliea and Luke stared at each other for a moment, smiles covering both of their faces when Cora coughed loudly.

"Well when you two love birds are done making googly eyes at each other, maybe we can actually go to the cafeteria and get food," She said haughtily.

"What!?" both of them seemed to say in unison.

"We're not dating…"

"It's not like that…"

"I'd never…"

"Woah woah woah, calm down," Conner said holding his hands up and waving them back and forth dramatically. "Cora was just kidding. Oh my god you guys can never tell the difference. Right sis?"

"Yeah chill. I wasn't being serious or

anything," She added looking between the two of them. "You guys are weird."

"Aww but that's why you love us," Luke said smiling and putting a hand on her shoulder.

"Yeah," Cora said, returning the grin. "That's why we love you."

"Alright this is getting too mushy," Emiliea interrupted. "Even for me."

"I see you haven't changed much in the last few weeks. Still as emotionally constipated as ever," Conner said with a laugh.

"I am not emotionally constipated," Emiliea gasped, shooting Conner an offended glance.

"That depends on the day," Cora agreed with her brother as they entered the food court. They moved through the food line quickly grabbing as much food as they could be allotted. After piling their plates sky high with food, the group made their way to an empty table in the middle of the cafeteria and began to eat.

"So you guys are graduating secondary this year right?" Emiliea asked. "Got any plans for the future?"

"Well Cora wants to stay here in Siberia, but I was thinking of going to the Antarctic village down south. I hear they still have Old World universities down there," Conner said excitedly. "I know it's not something people up here think is necessary but before we evacuated the Norwegian village to come up here, it was always a dream of mine."

"Well I think that's a great idea, Con," Emiliea said encouragingly.

"You would," Cora retorted anger coating her voice slightly. "But I've been trying to convince him for a while that staying up here is what's best for all of us."

"Come on Cora Antarctica can't be that bad," Conner argued. "I mean the other half of the human population is already living there."

"It's on the bottom of the globe. If

you move down there, we won't get to see you again," his sister replied, both of their voices growing more heated.

"Well excuse me for wanting to have a future," her brother growled. "I don't want to stay up here in this…"

Everyone at the table stared at him as he trailed off. He stayed frozen staring off at nothing, his eyes empty and vacant. His skin suddenly turned a few shades lighter and as the group realized what was happening the temperature seemed to drop a few degrees.

"Conner?" Cora hesitantly asked the worry in her voice causing it to shake slightly at the end.

The sound of his body hitting the floor would haunt all of them for the rest of their lives. Conner began convulsing violently, his eyes rolling back in his head. White foam began seeping out of his mouth where his teeth were crashing and grating against each other causing a harsh sound to fill the air with a sense of dread. Blue lines began to creep over his body in a spider web pattern covering his entire face and body. Blood began pouring out of his nose and ears pooling in a large red circle on the crisp white floor. Cora was screaming, holding her brother with tears running down her face trying to speak to him as his body revolted against him. Her clothes became red with blood and tear stains as Luke ran out yelling for someone to get the medics and healers. He turned back to the twins, trying to pry Cora from her brother's prone form making way for the doctors. All Emiliea could do was stare as one of her closest friends succumbed to the first stage of the Disease.

He was infected. And they all knew what that meant.

The medics came and whisked him away putting him on a stretcher and taking him to the Center Medical Unit. Cora followed her brother through the doors of the infirmary but Luke and

Emiliea were cut off by a guard in a white hazmat suit. A single drop of blood rested on his otherwise spotless uniform, though he seemed to take no notice of the red stain.

"Family members only," he said calmly as if it were no big deal that one of their best friends was dying. As if they weren't practically the only family that Cora and Conner had. They knew Conner would be dead within three to four days. The twins weren't rich. They worked hard and paid their own way through life and as much as she loved her brother, Cora wouldn't be able to afford keeping him alive for any longer. It's not that she wouldn't try, but the cost of life support was over $4,000 per day. They didn't even have that much money in the first place. If she sold everything that might buy her a single day. One more day to say goodbye before she was cast out into the streets like a wild animal. She'd have to become a Street Person.

The worst part about this was how much pain Conner would be in until his inevitable death. Currently, he was beginning phase one of the Disease. He would seize and bleed and sweat for hours while the whites of his eyes turned a rotten yellow color and his vision vanished. Blue lines would cover his body like the ancient markings of some long-lost civilization. Within 24 hours, he would enter phase two of the Disease. The blue lines would disappear from his skin and he would suffer from a high fever. Some people hallucinate during phase two, others just slept through it out of exhaustion. He would continue to bleed uncontrollably. The crimson liquid would pour out of every nook and cranny of his weakening body until he became ghastly pale.

By phase three, he'd be unrecognizable. His hair would fall from his head and his yellow eyes would gaze up at the ceiling, unable to blink. The pain he'd be in would be unimaginable.

There are those who killed themselves before they entered phase three to avoid what happened. The body was drained of all liquid. The skin shriveled up like an unwatered flower in the hot Siberian sun and all ability to function was lost as the body convulsed until it's last breath.

That was the fate that awaited Conner behind the Medical Unit doors. Emiliea let a tear fall from her face as she watched two of her best friends walk through the closed doors. This couldn't be real. It wasn't possible. And yet there she was clinging to Luke's shirt soaking it with sobs. He rubbed a hand on her back as they both walked over to the wall and sat down. Neither of them would be leaving the Center until they heard of Conner's condition or they saw Cora come out with news. Emiliea cried, the sound of her grief filling the busy hallways of the Center. Luke didn't shed a tear. He just gazed out into the distance, seemingly emotionless. To anyone passing by, they were just another family who lost someone to the Disease. Something that was becoming far too common for either of their tastes. They fell asleep like that, her laying her tearstained head on his soaked shoulder and him with his arms wrapped around her protectively as if trying to keep her safe from the horrors of their world.

When Emiliea woke up, the first thing she realized was that she wasn't at home. The place where she lay was hard and cold, unlike the warmth of her mattress and the comfort of her bedsheets. There were loud noises and bright lights which littered the atmosphere around her and were unfamiliar and strange. The second thing she noticed was that she was not alone. There was a pair of strong arms wrapped around her. They were warm, a sharp contrast to the cold tile beneath her. She breathed in, the scent of the person holding her was familiar, safe. But even though she felt secure in the hold, and even though she knew she was in no danger something still felt off, something was wrong.

Blinking she looked around to see that she was in the Center, near the medical wing it appeared. Medics were rushing in and out some of them covered in blood, others with scrubs which were spiffy clean. Her confusion only grew as she recognized where she was, and that confusion soon turned to panic. Was Kevin ok? The last time she'd been here, her brother had been given a mild treatment for Leukemia but no cure. Had it gotten so bad that doctors had to change their minds?

"Are you ok?" With the low voice of Luke from behind her, she began to remember the real reason she was lying on the floor without having changed her clothes. Conner. The Disease had struck again.

"No," she responded, her voice full of despair. Honestly, she wasn't sure she'd ever be ok again. She'd known

Conner for years, ever since he and Cora had escaped the ocean in Norway. He was always so sweet and kind. It wasn't fair that he was dying. It didn't make any sense either. Wasn't he fine less than a day ago? Hadn't she walked in on him and Cora doing their usual twin roughhousing in the VR room. They'd been joking around and teasing each other, having a good time. Why did this have to happen to him? To Cora? Maybe there was something she could have done. It was probably absurd to think she could've prevented his exposure, but maybe if she'd stayed home, if she'd stayed away from the center, he'd still be with his sister downstairs. Smiling and laughing without a care in the world.

"Emiliea, it's not your fault," Luke said as if reading her thoughts. She hated it when he did that but somehow, he always managed to figure out how to do it anyway.

"How do you know I'm blaming

myself?" she asked not moving at all. Her gaze was fixated on the floor as Luke shifted behind her moving so that he was looking at her face.

"I know you."

She looked up, her violet eyes capturing his baby blue ones. He did know her. Better than anyone else in the world. Out of the 2,400 people left on the planet, he was the only one she counted on when it mattered. Her own mother wasn't even on the list. She let a single tear fall down her cheek as she began to explain.

"You don't understand. It could be my fault. Maybe… maybe if I hadn't."

"Stop," he said, cutting her off. His eyes grew slightly angry for a moment as he continued. "Stop doing this to yourself Emi. Just because you happened to come to the Center doesn't mean anything. He could've been exposed before you even got here."

"That doesn't make it any easier."

His eyes softened.

"I know."

Emiliea sighed, closing her eyes and throwing her head back leaning against the wall. She took a series of deep breaths trying to control her emotions. It wouldn't do her any good to start crying now. Luke seemed to be doing the same thing, though a bit more successfully. Waiting was the worst part. It was like having to watch a movie about someone when you already knew the ending is tragic. There was something cruel about the world to force them to wait so long without any word on their friend. Another day passed without them having moved from that spot. They didn't eat or go home. They simply sat there refusing to leave their friend who most certainly wouldn't ever be doing those tasks again.

The news came early the next morning. An older looking nurse came out into the hall, his solemn face telling them everything they needed to know.

He only lasted two days.

"Did he make it to phase three?" Emiliea found herself asking. She regretted it almost instantly dreading whatever response the tired nurse would give her. When he shook his head, she wasn't sure whether to be relieved or devastated. She didn't know what to feel. Her head began spinning as she heard Luke let out a muffled cry behind her. A cold sensation began creeping up all her limbs making them feel like lead. Her knees began to buckle beneath her as she collapsed to the floor her entire person racked with trembling sobs.

From her spot on the ground she could hear the agonizing sound which pierced the air coming from behind the closed doors. The guttural scream that came from Cora could be heard all around the center. It echoed off of every wall filling the entire building with a sense of dread and fear. Death had struck again ripping another loved one away from the world and now everyone knew it. Cora must've just found out about her brother. There was no other reason for her to sound that way.

From behind her, Emiliea could feel Luke clenching and unclenching his fist as if wanting to punch the cause of all our pain. But you can't punch a disease. The rest of the world seemed blurred to them as they mourned their friend. They would never see him again. Funerals weren't held for those who died from the disease. Their bodies couldn't be exposed to such a large amount of people even if they were dead. Instead, healers burned the bodies to ash. They called it cremation, a practice which carried over from the Old World. After the bodies were burned, the remains were jettisoned into space. There was no closure for loved ones because the protection of the group was more important than the protection of feelings.

"Emi," Luke said, pulling her up off the ground. "Let's go, your mom is probably worried."

She knew that wasn't why he was pulling her away. He was trying to get them away from it all. From the Center, from the doctors. And most of all from the pungent reek of death that flooded the rooms. She didn't have the energy to protest, so she let him lead her away. They walked calmly out of the Center both of them trying to keep their emotions within themselves. They couldn't break down, not there. The force of the full sun was beating down on them harshly, causing them to sweat profusely as they walked past the street people. Just as they were reaching the edge of the street, Emiliea screamed as someone yanked the headwrap off her head. She quickly turned around punching her assailant in the face.

"What the hell?" she asked as Luke came to stand behind her. The person who'd attempted to steal from them was an older woman, a street person. She was now cowering on the ground looking up at the two passerbyers.

"I'm sorry, I just needed the money," she begged, holding her hands up over her face. Her whole body was shaking in desperation. "I need it, my child is dying, please, he doesn't have much time."

"I'm sorry," Emiliea responded sympathetically, "I don't have any money on me."

"Please," the old woman cried. "I'm trying to get to the Central Regions. There is a cure there. In the old ruins left by the ancient Old World natives. I can save him. Please you have to help me."

"Mam, we don't have any money," Luke reiterated. "I hope you are able to save your son, but we can't help." Emiliea hid a tear as it trickled down her face. She knew this woman was delusional. There was no cure for the disease. It didn't exist. She was only growing delusional because of what was happening to her son. Trembling with sorrow, Emiliea turned away with Luke walking closely behind. They had only taken a few steps when the woman screamed in anger, throwing the headwrap back at the pair.

"You are all monsters! All of you who live up there pretending you're saving the human race by not risking contamination. Why can't you save my son? His life is worth more than any of you bastards who die in that metal can in the village."

"You have no idea what's going on in there," Luke yelled back angrily. He turned around and grabbed Emiliea's hand pulling her behind him as they exited the street.

By the time they reached the outskirts of the village, they began to run. Running was something they used to do a lot when they were kids. Before the fall of the third village, the one where Conner and Cora had come from, they could run all the time. It was always so freeing to feel the wind in their hair and the air rushing past the faces.

Neither of those things were happening now. Now they weren't running for fun. Emiliea couldn't feel the wind in her hair and the air around them seemed to be suffocating them not liberating them. But even though they felt trapped by the feeling of their marathon, they didn't stop. The steel trap of the Center was far worse than the one they were creating themselves. They ran until they couldn't see the modern building on the horizon anymore. It was miles away from any place civilized but the best part about that was how isolated they were from the rest of the world. Out here, they could just pretend nothing else existed.

Soon, the sandy terrain of the desert began to convert into the tall canopy of trees that was the forest. They stopped there. No one was really allowed in the forest except for the workers who trekked back and forth to bring water to the community. They were both hunched over breathing heavily to recover from the long run. The sun glistened in the sky as they made their way over to a fallen tree and sat down. The entire environment was silent, with the exception of the rasping of the two best friends. Neither of them knew what to say to each other after losing one of their oldest companions. Though it had only been a few days since Conner's diagnosis, both of them seemed to have aged decades. The haunted look in their eyes resembled elders who had lost far more than they should have. It was unnatural to see the result of so much death on their young faces.

"What happens now?" Luke asked, staring out into the distance. He seemed broken, as if the weight of the world rested on his shoulders. Emiliea shrugged the same blank expression painting her features. She knew she should feel exhausted from the events of the past week, but she didn't feel anything. She tried to move but she couldn't find the motivation nor the energy to. Instead the only thing she felt was numb. It was a cool and paralyzing sensation which terrified her, it chilled her to the bone. But even though the lack of sensation petrified her, she still couldn't do a thing. Luke seemed to sense her unresponsiveness because he waited a while before speaking again.

"I feel like a terrible person," he confessed, grasping her hand in his. When she still didn't move, he continued. "I keep thinking about what happened. And Conner, he was like a little brother to me but, I keep thinking how grateful I am that it wasn't you."

Emiliea finally mustered the strength to look up at her childhood friend as she observed him sniffle and wipe his eyes.

"Does that make me a bad person?" he asked brokenly. She stared at him unable to think of an appropriate response. She knew it was wrong to be happy it was someone else. That selfishness is what drove the Old World to the brink of destroying the planet forcing the few that survived to live wary of everything. It's the reason they were an endangered species in the first place. But at the same time, she couldn't help but feel the same way. The mere thought of that was enough to dread up fear in her heart. How could she even think that? One life was not worth more than any other, and it was dangerous to consider otherwise. At the same time, did that not mean that the lives of the street people should matter just as much as the ones who resided in the Center? Or the ones who chose to live apart from the village like her, Angela, and Kevin?

It didn't make any sense. The hypocrisy of the healers to say that no one was special and yet treat some like royalty and others like a piece of worthless crap. Why shouldn't she value the ones closest to her more than those who were complete strangers? She loved

Kevin and his death was devastating. But if Luke or Kevin died? She'd be completely obliterated by the loss.

"No," she settled on saying. She didn't know if she completely believed that, but then again, she never was sure of anything. And telling Luke he was evil because he didn't want her to die was wrong, that much she knew for sure.

"Do you ever wonder how much time we have left?" he said randomly, closing his eyes. "I mean look at the world. We both know at least ten people who have died in the last six months."

"I try not to think about it," Emiliea replied honestly. "I don't want to."

"It's just, I can't believe that on any given day either one of us could wake up with the other rotting from blood loss or being burned to ash."

"Luke, please. Don't say something like that. I couldn't survive that."

"Emi, this is important. It's not like we have much of a choice! The Disease is just going to keep on infecting, torturing, and killing. I don't want that to happen without saying goodbye. If I'm going to die, I want it to be with no regrets."

"Please," Emiliea grunted. "Stop. It's bad enough that Conner is dead. I refuse to lose you or Kevin too. I won't. Somehow, we will beat this. It doesn't matter what it costs."

"That's a mistake. Not everyone is worth the cost. Especially if you don't know what it will do to you when you pay it. I'm certainly not worth it."

"You will always be worth it. You and Kev are the only reasons I'm here right now. God knows nothing else about life here has an appeal. We can talk about this, but just…" she trailed off imagining what Conner must've looked like in those last few moments. She wondered if he'd been screaming in pain or enduring vivid hallucinations. Hesitantly, she tried to force herself to picture Luke or Kevin in his place. She tried to picture either of them broken and covered in red as blood continued to gush from their ears. "Just later," she finished in a whisper.

Luke nodded as if he understood what she was saying, before standing up and offering her his hand. She looked at it questioningly moving her head to meet his steady gaze.

"Come on," he said, pulling her up. "I'll walk you home."

"It's ok, you don't have to," Emiliea began to protest before he cut her off.

"I want to."

Slowly she nodded and the two began their silent journey to her home. They didn't speak again simply trying to enjoy each other's company, but Luke's suggestion floated around in her head threatening her sanity and plaguing her entire being with worry and paranoia. She tried not to let it show as they approached the steps to the quaint cottage where she lived. She began to ascend when she heard Luke yell from behind her.

"Stay safe, Emi. And come by the Center again soon."

"I will," she yelled after him as he started to walk away. "I promise."

She stayed on the stairway, watching as he faded into the distance, nothing more than a speck of black on the hazy horizon. The sun was setting, so with a long and weary sigh, she gathered herself and opened the front door. The decontamination room smelled strongly of cleaning products. The harsh stench assaulting her nostrils as she entered causing her to become nauseous. She nearly gagged at the overwhelming scent. Closing the front door behind her, she reached back and unclasped the hook which fastened her scarf in place around her neck. The feeling of the weight of fabric being lifted nearly made her fall over in relief.

Setting the scarf aside, she began to take off her sweater and boots and pants. The hot air felt cool against her sweat-soaked skin. The thin tank top and short shorts she was left in clung to her body like saran wrap, the dampness of her figure keeping the fabric sticking to her like a strong glue. She felt better and worse at the same time, knowing that she was back in the safety of her secluded home. Walking over to the touchpad by the entryway, she typed in her password and entered the cleansing chamber. Within seconds she felt the chamber closing and the room being filled with disinfectants and cleaners. She coughed as the mist of chemicals filled the air and squinted her eyes to avoid the mixture from entering them. Even though the process was less than a minute, it still felt painfully long.

It always felt like she was burning. It was as if her skin was lit on fire and she had no choice but to endure it just so that she could enter her own home. When the process was over, she sucked in a deep breath as the door finally opened and let her in. As soon as she stepped out into the foyer, she found small arms wrapping around her body. Kevin had thrown his arms around his sister excitedly jumping up and down.

"Where were you? I was so worried," he asked, clinging to her tightly. And despite everything that had happened since she'd left, she couldn't help but smile as she returned the embrace wrapping her arms around him in a big hug.

"I'm ok, Kev, I'm ok," she said softly, kneeling down so she could be at his eye-level.

"Mom said something happened at the Center. Asinus told her," he told her restricting his grip even more. "Someone was infected, and I thought it was you."

"It wasn't. See," Emiliea responded standing up and turning around as if to show him. "I'm perfectly ok."

"Who was it?"

She blanched when he asked her that. It was such an innocent question too.

He had no idea that the victim, the newest corpse on the pile waiting to be burned, was one of her best friends. How could he? Kevin for his part seemed to immediately understand that it wasn't something his older sister had any desire to talk about.

"It's ok," he assured her when she didn't respond. "You don't have to tell me. But I'm here for you anyway."

Emiliea nodded and smiled trying to portray her gratefulness without speaking, she wasn't sure anything would come out even if she tried. Her little brother gave her a small pat on the back and even that small action brought her great comfort. Clearing her throat, she looked around realizing her mother wasn't in the living room.

"Where's Angela?" she asked, although she was worried that she already knew the answer. Sure enough, Kevin gestured to the room behind them.

"She hasn't been out since she heard

about the, umm, incident at the Center."

Emiliea sighed before placing her hand on Kevin's cheek.

"Why don't you go upstairs and freshen up to get ready for bed," She suggested. "We can have a movie night just like old times while Mom sleeps it off."

Kevin began nodding excitedly, his glasses nearly falling off his face as he raced upstairs. She smiled as he went, before frowning as she approached the room her mother was in.

"Angela," she yelled from outside hoping, to no avail that she would answer without any other prompt. When the house continued to stay silent, Emiliea repressed a wave of anger and opened the door. Photos littered the floor of her mother's bedroom as she walked in. The prominent figures in all of them were a young woman and a man. They looked happy and carefree in almost every picture.

Continuing her way into the dirty

room, Emiliea saw empty bottles on every surface. Broken glass shards were creating a dangerous obstacle course and she cursed as a sharp piece sliced the bottom of her foot. Drawing in a sharp breath she ignored it. It stunk like alcohol and depression inside as she finally saw the drunken form of her mother sitting on the floor. Her back was pushed up against a bed frame, her legs sprawled out in front of her as she stared out distantly with a glazed over look in her eyes. Emiliea wanted to scream as she saw her mom like that. Even though it's what she expected it still hurt to know that Kevin had probably been abandoned and alone for all that time. Walking over to Angela, she pulled her up from her place on the ground and threw her unceremoniously under the covers.

Her mother groaned as she settled down allowing her daughter to pull the sheets over her. She would be hungover in the morning, but Emiliea didn't find it in herself to care at the moment. After completing that task, she left and went to the washroom. She bandaged her newly injured foot, wincing as she put rubbing alcohol on the cut. The cut wasn't too deep, so hopefully it would heal in the next few days. Next, she took a hairbrush and began to untangle the brown locks, it took her numerous attempts before she simply gave up and exited out to the living room. Kevin was already there waiting for her, popcorn in hand as she cued up some Old World action movie about teenagers being trapped in a jungle-themed game. It was somewhat interesting, but she found it to be entirely unrealistic and strange.

Kevin began yawning about halfway through the movie and by the time the credits rolled he was fast asleep on the other side of the couch. Emiliea looked over at his sleeping form with an unknown emotion burning in her chest. He looked so peaceful like this, so young and unafraid of the world. Happy too. In fact, he looked more alive and content in his sleep than in real life. She wondered what he was dreaming about that made him so cheerful. His lips were slightly curved upwards, the ghost of a smile dancing across his face. She wished she could keep him like that forever, happy. Not having to deal with the burdens that came with life, no matter how short that might end up being.

Emiliea allowed a single tear to fall down her face. Almost nothing in this hellish world made any sense but looking at her little brother she knew there was one thing that always would. She would protect Kevin at all costs. No matter what happened to her, or to Angela, she would always be there to help him out with whatever he needed. A large bang shook her away from her thoughts, making her turn her head to try and find the source of the noise. Another crash confirmed what she'd already suspected. Angela was awake.

She was most definitely hung over if the ruckus that she had caused was anything to go by. Emiliea gave one last long look at her brother before standing up and making her way over to where her mom was just entering the kitchen.

Angela's hair was messy, although she seemed to take no notice as she loudly opened the door into the icebox. She pulled out a can of beer and opened it, chugging it down. Her daughter stared at her incredulously.

"Mom, what the hell?" She asked angrily, her eyes burning with fury. Her mom immediately dropped the can looking up at her in shock.

"Oh, thank god," she said shakily, bringing a hand up to her forehead. "I thought you might have been infected. You didn't come home for days and the last time that happened was because you were in quarantine."

"As if you'd actually care," Emiliea retorted crossing her arms. Angela looked up with a dangerous look in her eyes as her daughter continued. "I came back and you were drunk and high while Kevin was left to fend for himself. I thought we were past this, mom. You promised me this would stop."

"Don't you dare," Angela growled back, placing her shaking hands firmly on the counter although it was unclear if that was to steady her swaying body or to appear intimidating. "First of all, Kevin is absolutely fine so I don't understand why you're bitching so much about something that's none of your damn business. You don't get to come home and judge me for having a few drinks."

"A few drinks? Mom, you were passed out from alcohol poisoning. I found your unconscious body on the floor with dozens of open bottles cracked open around you. That isn't a few drinks. I mean… shit what if Kevin had had a stroke or something while you were out drinking booze or popping pills or whatever the hell it is you were doing to try and make yourself feel good."

"Don't act so innocent you ungrateful child. I sent you to the Center to get milk. That shouldn't be too difficult. Instead, you go missing for days without calling or sending a messenger. Then I heard that someone collapsed and was dying. Do you have any idea how difficult that was for me?"

"Considering it was my friend who died, yeah. Let's say I have an idea. And yet here I am, completely sober and awake. I could smell his rotting corpse from the hallways while you were sitting on your ass letting your son die of dehydration and starvation. Thank god I taught him how to take his own medication otherwise I would have had to say goodbye to two people I love this week," Emiliea retorted her voice cracking at the end. "I thought this part of our lives was over. I thought I was done coming home to a house that smelled like liquor. It's been weeks since the last time you drank. I thought we were finally in a good place. And then on the one day, the one day I needed to come home to someone to support me I have to fix your messes. Again."

"Am I supposed to feel sorry for you?" Angela spat. "I've lost people too."

"Dad isn't dead!" Emiliea screamed. "He was alive last time I checked. You drove him away with all your drugs and drinks. Alcohol was more important than him, so he left. And in case you had forgotten, you weren't the only one he left. He left me here too. With you. I'll never forgive him for that."

"I didn't drive your father away. He loved me and I loved him. He wouldn't do that to me."

"Yes, you did. And you've lived in denial for ten years since. I've been raising my brother for ten years. Do you have any idea how much I have sacrificed?"

"Don't make this about you! Nobody

asked you to do anything."

"Well excuse me if I decided that I wasn't going to sit by and watch my brother die."

Angela stared at her daughter contemplatively before rolling her eyes and taking another long swig of her beverage and throwing the empty glass bottle on the ground. Emiliea shook her head disgusted before turning around and storming out of the room. Storming up the stairs, she tried to be as quiet as possible so that Kevin wouldn't wake up. This was impossible, she couldn't live like this anymore. There was too much pressure and responsibility weighing down on her that she was practically drowning.

The door slammed behind her causing a loud echo to resound through the large old house. Had she thrown it any harder it may have even split the wood in two. As it was, the whole house shook and Emiliea winced slightly as she recalled Kevin sleeping downstairs, but she couldn't bring herself to check. This was all too much to deal with. Kevin's sickness, Angela's absence both emotionally and physically, and now Conner's death. One of her best friends.

She didn't understand how her mother could be so cruel after that kind of event. Even though no one she knew had model parents, with Cora and Conner being orphans and Luke's dad being an abusive bastard, she had always hoped things would change. Watching Old World tv shows, it seemed like it was possible. But life had taught her a different lesson. Her mother lied to her, broke her promise, and nearly cost her the life of her little brother. There would be no change of heart or growth of character. She couldn't look up to her mom as a good person, she couldn't turn a blind eye to the selfish and self-destructive personality her mother embodied. No matter how many times she tried to talk to her mom or communicate, she didn't change. No one ever could. The only person she could rely on was herself. No one else would ever stick their neck out to save hers.

Emiliea shuddered as she took a deep breath, the stench of alcohol entering her nose. The smell clung to her clothes making her want to gag or puke. Tears began to stream down her face as she gasped for breath desperately trying to remain calm and breathe. But it wasn't working. She had to get this wretched odor off of her body. Grabbing a set of sleepwear and a hairbrush, she quietly slipped over to the bathroom across the hall. A loud creak signified the rusty hinges managing to open the door wide enough for her to fit inside. The old room was dark and dusty with a pungent smell and a cracked floor. A shiver ran down her spine as she entered but she set her things down on the odd-looking white seat and searched for the light switch. The sudden flash of brightness blinded her causing her to shield her eyes away from the source on the ceiling. She quickly flipped the lights back off, ending the assault on her vision.

Sighing, she resigned herself to the dark as she began stripping off her clothes, peeling the damp tank top and shorts off and letting herself enjoy the feeling of nothingness. She was about to step into the tub when she realized that she'd forgotten something. The headwrap was still securely stationed on top of her head. Slowly, she walked over and stood in front of the mirror glancing at herself in the reflection. She almost didn't recognize the girl staring back at her. Her eyes were surrounded by redness and dried tears. The pinkness of her puffy cheeks was obvious even through her dark skin. Her violet eyes held an extra layer of sadness that she knew from others would never leave her.

She reached a hand out to touch the mirror, almost wishing it was a different person and that the life she would return to outside this room would be different. But that couldn't happen. This was who she was and her life would not be changing anytime soon. Shakily, she redirected her hand to the back of her head. Her fingers struggled to find the clasp which held her hair in place but after a few tries, the old fabric fell away from her head gently. Her hair, which only days ago had been full and vibrant, seemed to match the dull tone of the room. Even though the headwrap was gone, the greasy locks seemed to stay in the same place, stubbornly, not wanting to move. The brown color was almost black in the shadows of the old room. Before she could see anything else in her reflection, she took a towel from the side cabinet and threw it over the mirror. There was nothing she wanted to see in it anyway.

Her movements were sluggish as she stepped into the tub. Although she knew what she was doing was wrong, self-indulgence was something that was never permitted at the Center, she couldn't help but feel a rush of happiness as the cold water rushed over her skin. It was thrilling. But she knew that before she could relax she had to get the smell of hooch off her skin. Grabbing a small bar of soap, she began to scrub. She scrubbed for what seemed like hours and yet the smell lingered so she scrubbed harder. She scrubbed and scrubbed and scrubbed until the muscles in her arm began to ache and the skin of the area she was trying to clean turned red and raw. When she was done, she just sat there in the water. She knew eventually she'd have to get up and leave, but for now, she was going to ensure this moment lasted as long as possible.

A loud crash and scream were what woke her up. She gasped and shot upright causing the water around her to splash out of the tub and onto the floor. At first, Emiliea couldn't even remember where she was. The darkness of the room covering every inch of her surroundings made it impossible for her to decipher what the objects around her were. However, there weren't many rooms in the house that would have large quantities of water. As soon as she realized where she was a pang of guilt coursed through her mind. How could she have been so wasteful? What had she been thinking that led her to waste gallons and gallons of water on something as tedious as a warm bath?

Another wail from downstairs caused her to temporarily abandon her self loathing and quickly step out of the tub. She dried herself and threw on the clothes she'd brought in with her the night before. Her headwrap was the last thing she went to grab, but her hand only descended onto an empty shelf. Confusion passed through her but she shrugged it off and simply wrapped her hair in a towel so that it would dry. She raced out of the dimly lit room pushing the slightly cracked door open and bounding down the stairs two at a time. When she reached the bottom, she looked around for the source of the noise and nearly fell over at the sight in front of her. A scream tore out of her throat painfully as she took in the scene.

Kevin was lying in a pool of his own blood the red contrasting against the paleness of his skin. It was staining his once white hair while blue lines covered his face and hands. His convulsing form seemed almost lifeless despite the fact that she'd never seen him move so much at once. Emiliea couldn't move. In her mind she was rushing forward to help her brother, she was calling the Center to get a Medic. But in reality she was crumpling to the ground in sheer shock. This couldn't be happening, not to Kevin. She crawled forward slowly, not caring about the chances of her receiving the disease. If Kevin got it, it didn't matter whether she lived or died, her life would be over either way.

After too long, his body stilled and his eyes began to drift close. A tear fell down her cheek as she tapped him gently. All she wanted to see was his eyes to open. Even just a little flutter of his eyelids. But he remained completely still, to the point that he could have been mistaken for a corpse marked for the incinerator. A gentle pull on her arm caused her to look up and see the blank mask of a hazmat suit. The man was pulling her away from the prone form of Kevin, despite her desperate attempts to stay with him. She had clearly been with him for a while if her mother had found them and called the Center, but everything seemed to be moving too fast. The world was being interpreted as flashes of events and not as passing time.

They took Kevin. She knew that she had to leave and find them. Surely they would let her come and stay with him, but she couldn't bring her wobbly legs to support her. She teetered and fell each time she tried. The world around her was blurry at the edges as she continued crawling towards the pool of blood in the center of the room. The entire room was drenched in the metallic smell of iron and she almost retched as the putrid scent of alcohol and crimson liquid mixed in the air. She let out a small whimper as her hand slipped out from under her when it pressed down on a piece of red soaked fabric. Looking down she took the cloth in her hands as the blood continued to seep into the floorboards. It looked familiar, but it was almost impossible to discern the original color. She continued to look at it, almost as if she was hoping it would somehow reveal the answer to everything.

Emiliea wasn't sure how long she stayed there, curled up in on herself, sobbing. But the next thing she remembered was someone shaking her shoulder trying to get her attention. None of this was fair. Why did this have to happen to Kevin of all people? It didn't make any sense, how could he have gotten infected? They'd taken all the necessary precautions, and then some. Angela may have been a horrible mother, but that doesn't mean she never cared. Especially in the weeks when she was sober she implemented family rules. No one should have been able to contaminate the house.

"Emi, get up."

She tried to move but it felt as though there were weights keeping her down on the floor. Instead she collapsed and began to sob. Kevin was her whole world. She couldn't do this without him. His being there was the main reason she came home at night and didn't run off like her father did. A blanket of warmth enveloped her as arms wrapped around her shaking frame, pulling her closer to someone's chest.

"Emi we gotta go. Kev is already in the medical wing."

Emiliea looked up sadly at the person

who was giving her a large embrace. Luke met her gaze softly, his red-rimmed eyes glistening with unshed tears. A large purple bruise marked the right side of his face. Slowly, she nodded letting him support her as they rose to their feet unsteadily. As they made their way outside, she looked back at the Old World building she'd called a home for almost her whole life knowing that whatever happened with Kevin, this was the last time she would ever step foot in the run-down house.□

PART TWO: QUEST FOR THE CURE

Emiliea paced in the sterile white hallways of the Center. She and Luke had been there for two days now, and even though Kevin had stabilized as much as possible, he had still progressed into the second stage of the disease. The doctors had promised to give her an update as soon as possible but it had been over four hours and she was beginning to get desperate. There had to be a way to save her brother. They must be missing something. Maybe there was some medication they hadn't tried yet.

"Emi, calm down. I'm sure they're doing everything they can," Luke said as she continued to walk rapidly back and forth in the hallway.

"There has to be something else," she replied anxiously. "I just don't understand. He shouldn't have even been able to get it. I was so careful it doesn't make any sense."

"I don't know," Luke responded equally confused. "I mean you went through the decontamination room right?"

Emiliea nodded. "There shouldn't have been a way for the disease to get into the house."

"Well did he touch anything before he got infected?"

Emiliea thought back to when she'd found Kevin on the floor. At the time, he'd been holding onto a stained piece of cloth.

"He was holding onto some fabric," she said hesitantly.

"Can I see it?"

Emiliea nodded walking over to her backpack that she'd brought and opened it up. Grabbing the stained object she handed it to him and he looked over it critically.

"Emi, this is your headwrap," he said slowly looking up at her with an unreadable expression.

"What? No, no that's not right. I had it with me when I went upstairs. It was right…" Emiliea trailed off. No. The door had been open when she'd woken up in the bath. No. She hadn't grabbed her headwrap before she'd rushed downstairs. No. She found him curled up with it just like how he always did when he was little. No. No. No. No. No. No. This couldn't be true. She began hyperventilating and even as her head began to feel light she couldn't stop. This was her fault. If she'd been more careful. That woman yesterday, the street person, she'd stolen her headwrap and contaminated it. And then Emiliea practically gave it to Kevin.

"Shhhh," Luke soothed as she continued to sob. "Shhh… it'll be ok. We'll figure it out."

Emiliea shook her head softly.

"Luke, there's nothing to figure out. He's already dead there is no cure for the disease."

"There has to be something we can do," he argued.

She continued shaking her head. No one in the Center had ever survived before. Not long term.

Emiliea thought back to yesterday, to the woman that had practically sentenced Kevin to death. She was so desperate for money so that she could… she was going to find a cure. In the Central Regions. She'd thought the Old World's ancient civilizations down there held the key to saving her son. It was ridiculous, but what if she was right? What if there was a cure down there. Shouldn't she at least try?

"What are you thinking?" Luke asked, noticing the look on her face.

"What if that street person was telling the truth?" she asked breathily. "What if there is a cure?"

"No she was crazy. There's no way."

"Even if there is a slight chance I have to try."

"That's a terrible idea, how will you even get to the Central Regions? You don't even know what you're looking for."

"But someone does," Emiliea said standing up. She sprinted down the hall stopping at the end as she saw Angela walk in. They stared at each other awkwardly before Angela spoke.

"Is he ok?" Her weak trembling voice shocked the pair. Emiliea looked up at her mother with wet eyes and shook her head. Angela seemed to understand as she sniffled and walked over to a bench. She sat down tiredly and looked up at her daughter. "Where are you going?" she asked, noticing her proximity to the door.

"I can save Kevin," Emiliea responded immediately. "I met someone yesterday. She can take us to a cure in the Central Regions."

"The Central Regions?" Angela asked incredulously. "No Emiliea don't. You'll die there."

"If I stay here, and do nothing then it doesn't matter. Mom, I have to try."

"I don't want to lose you too," her mother responded sadly.

Emiliea walked up to her mother and kneeled down in front of her pulling her shaking body into a tight embrace. "You won't." She said firmly. "But I have to go."

With that Emiliea turned and began walking away.

"Tell them to keep Kevin alive until I get back," Emiliea added. "I'm going to save him."

Angela nodded as she watched her daughter and Luke walk out the doors, a tear slipping from her eye.

"So what's your plan here, Emi?"

Luke asked finally. "I mean we told the truth yesterday, we don't have any money."

"We don't need any," She responded with a slight smirk. Luke raised an eyebrow at her response. "You'll see."

"Ok as long as you know what you're doing," he responded.

"Please, I always know what I'm doing."

"That's debatable," came a voice from behind them. The pair turned away to see Cora standing behind them.

"How much did you hear?" Emiliea asked nervously.

"All of it. I'm coming with you."

"Absolutely not," Luke said aggressively.

"Cora you just lost your brother," Emiliea reasoned.

"Exactly, I have nothing to lose.

You guys are the only family I have left so wherever you go, so do I."

Luke and Emiliea looked at each other worriedly, before Cora rolled her eyes and walked past them.

"I wasn't asking," she said over her shoulder. "Now let's get our tour guide and get the hell out of here."

Emiliea sighed knowing there was no way to convince her to stay. She gestured to Luke and they began walking leaving the Center behind them. Within minutes, they'd made their way to the streets and began looking around for the street person from the day before. They found her with a small boy wrapped in a blood-red cloth inside an Old World drug store. She looked up at them as they approached.

"Who was it?" she asked softly a distant look in her eyes. The group looked at each other warily before Emiliea stepped forward.

"My brother," she said shakily. "I wasn't lying yesterday. I don't have any money. I don't have a plane either. But I have a plan. If you help us, then maybe we can save your son."

A broken look passed over the woman's face.

"My son is already dead," she whispered hoarsely. "Everyone I loved is."

Luke walked up to her slowly and looked at the boy in red that was cradled in her arms. His eyes were still open, but they stared lifelessly into the distance. The blanket they thought was red, was simply stained in blood. It was still damp as Luke knelt down and closed the boy's eyes.

"I'm so sorry," he said to the

woman quietly.

"There was nothing you could have done," she responded, putting a hand on his shoulder. "I will help you save your brother. I couldn't save my own son, but I can save him."

"Thank you," Emiliea responded. The woman nodded before pulling the blanket over her son's head and putting him down in the store.

"We must go quickly if he has already been infected," The woman said and Emiliea nodded.

"Follow me."

They walked for a good while until they reached a large field guarded by three people. They crouched down behind a bush as Emiliea shushed them. She pointed to a small plane on the edge of the field.

"Get in and start the engine.

Luke, do you know how to fly one of those things?"

"Yeah I can get it in the air," he responded. "But what about you?"

"I'll be right there. Wait for my signal," she responded before taking off in the opposite direction. She made her way to the other side of the field as quickly as possible. Her plan was simple. Distract the guards so her friends could steal the plane and then try not to get caught while she boarded. Now that she was thinking about it, maybe it wasn't so simple. But it was all she had. She took a deep breath before grabbing a rock from the ground, aiming, and hurling at a guard's head. The rock hit its mark as the guard screamed and crumpled to the ground. The other two turned quickly just in time to see Emiliea throw another projectile at their heads. It missed both times and now she had the attention of both of them behind her. She turned around and ran.

She went about a minute into the forest before quickly switching directions and moving to go back to the field. Her lungs were burning with exertion when she arrived but she smiled when she saw the plane beginning to make its way across. With a final burst of energy, she sprinted toward the plane jumping on just as the guards made their way out of the brush. They were screaming at the group to stop, but Luke simply pulled the controls down and the plane began to gain altitude.

"Way to go," Cora said smiling as she collapsed on the inside of the aircraft.

"Thanks," Emiliea responded, trying to catch her breath.

"Here," the street person said coming forward with a small bag of water. "Drink."

Emiliea happily complied, chugging down the whole bag.

"I never asked," she said when she was finished. "What's your name?"

"Eliza" the woman replied with a gentle smile. "My name is Eliza."

"I'm Emiliea."

Eliza nodded and sat down across from the girl.

"What can you tell me about the cure?" Emiliea asked suddenly. "You said it was in the Central Regions but what is it exactly?"

"Well I'm not sure what it is. But when I was young, I studied the history of the Old World. It was terrible. I remember reading all the atrocities we committed against each other back then and it is awful. I do not understand how anyone could have behaved like this. One act of violence fascinated me however. It was an old civilization, even older than what we consider to be the Old World. They called them the Aztecs. When the people of Europe began to cross over the oceans, they brought with them many diseases. However none were quite as deadly as La Fiebre Sangrienta. The illness destroyed whole cities within days. It was described as leaving the victims with a fever bleeding until their inevitable death. However, there was one city where they developed a cure. It fell only months later when the Spaniards came and conquered it and no one ever saw the disease or the cure again."

"And you think that this disease, La Fiebre Sangrienta, is the same one that killed almost seven billion people?" Cora asked sitting next to Emiliea.

"I do. If we can find the fallen city, we will be able to get the formula. I can read many Old World languages, I will be able to translate it."

"Emi you can't seriously believe that," Cora exclaimed loudly. "This sounds like an old bedtime story."

"This is the only chance Kevin has," Emiliea argued back. "Cora, if you could go back, if this were Conner, what would you do?"

"Look I'm not saying we shouldn't try, but we have no plan. We don't even know where to start looking."

"In Mexico, the Old World country. That's where the city was,"

Eliza responded.

"Even so, Mexico is a big country. How do we know exactly where to land?" Cora asked.

"So we narrow it down. Were there any other descriptions of the fallen city?"

"Umm, it was surrounded by mountains and it was on the water."

"Well that narrows it down to the center of the country. There weren't quite as many mountains on the coasts," Emiliea pointed out.

"What was the climate like? Was it hot or cold?"

"It was warmer. But why does that matter?"

"It's always warmer near the equator, so now we know it's in the southern part of the country. The question is where exactly is it located."

"Well we could land at the

bottom and make our way up to the top," Cora suggested.

"That may take too long. By that time, Kevin will already be dead."

"What if we landed at the first sign of a lake and then spread out from there?" Eliza asked. "That would be quicker and we could always go back into the plane if we need to."

"Ok that sounds better. I'll let Luke know," Emiliea said, making her way to the cockpit. Luke looked almost peaceful up in the cabin of the plane alone. She felt kind of bad about disturbing him.

"Did you guys figure out where we are going?" Luke asked looking up at her as she entered.

"Southern part of the Old World Mexico. We are looking for mountains with lakes," Emiliea responded. "Supposedly the cure is in some ancient city."

"Yeah, we'll see I guess," Luke responded. He noticed how Emiliea seemed to droop with some unnamable emotion. "Are you ok?"

"Just tired," she tried but sighed in resignation when she saw Luke's disbelieving look. "I'm worried about Kevin. I mean he's got his entire life out ahead of him he can't… I can't lose him."

"And you won't," Luke said kindly. "Emi, we're gonna find the cure and we are going to save your brother, I promise."

"You shouldn't make promises you can't keep."

"And you shouldn't be so pessimistic. We have a real shot at getting this cure. Don't give up hope yet."

"I won't, but you shouldn't get your hopes up either."

"Well someone has to look on the positive side around here," Luke said, smirking. "What with all the doom and gloom stuff you've been talking about recently."

Emiliea rolled her eyes and settled into the copilot's chair closing her eyes. It was going to be a long flight.

Hours passed before they reached the southern part of Mexico. The atmosphere of the plane was heavy as everyone began peering out the windows searching for any sign of the fallen city. They flew relatively close to the ground in order to see the outside world.

"There," Emiliea said pointing to a small plot of land in the distance. "Surrounded by mountains and in the center is a lake. That matches the description."

"Ok I'll set us down," Luke said,

pulling the plane down.

The group made their way outside, the hot sun beating down on them causing sweat to roll down their faces.

"God, it feels like I'm melting," Cora complained, wiping droplets off her forehead.

"Yeah I thought Siberia was hot," Luke agreed.

"Come on guys, the faster we find the fallen city the faster we can go home and save my brother," Emiliea said pushing past them, Eliza following closely behind.

She walked up to the lake, taking in the sight of the gorgeous water sparkling in the sunlight. Looking down, she could see small fish swimming near the shoreline.

"This place is beautiful," she said looking around. Luke came up behind her as she stared in the water.

"Yeah, it really is," he said smiling. Emiliea smiled back feeling a bit lighter than she had earlier.

"I think it's this way," Eliza said, walking behind them. "Come on."

"Yeah you guys can have your makeout session when we get home," Cora added laughing.

"What?" "That wasn't what,"

"Wow you were right they are touchy about that," Eliza said, turning to Cora who threw her head back trying to muffle her laughter.

"I know right."

"You have got to stop doing that," Emiliea said frustratedly.

"I agree. It's embarrassing," Luke added.

"Not for me it's not," Cora responded.

They walked further and further into the jungle, but to no avail.

Emiliea looked around angrily. This was her one chance to find this cure. Without it, Kevin would die.

"Emi, come over here!" Luke shouted. Emiliea turned around, jogging over to where Luke was standing.

"What is it?" she asked, coming to stand next to him. He pointed towards the edge of a mountain and walked towards it.

"Look here. The stone is uneven."

Emiliea walked closer to inspect it. She ran her hand over the rock feeling for anything out of place. She stopped when she felt a crack in the stone. Curious, she pushed down on it. She jumped back as the rock swung open to reveal a door. She looked over at Luke, eyes wide. He too seemed to be surprised.

"Holy crap," Cora said running

up behind them.

"It's real," Eliza said stunned.

Emiliea nodded, starstruck, before turning back to face everyone.

"You three need to stay here," she said firmly. The protest that followed was deafening.

"Absolutely not Emi. We're coming with you," Luke half yelled.

"I agree with Luke here. There is no way in hell you're doing this alone," Cora agreed.

"Emiliea, it could be dangerous," Eliza added.

"I know. That's why I have to go alone."

"No way," Luke protested again. "You are not leaving me here. What if something happens in there?"

"Then you three will be alive and that's all that matters."

"No. I'm coming with you."

Emiliea glared frustratedly at Luke before letting out an angry sigh.

"Fine," she agreed. "But Cora and Eliza stay here."

"What no way," Cora began, but Emiliea interrupted.

"Or I go alone."

Cora and Eliza glared before Eliza responded.

"Deal. But be safe Emiliea."

"I will, I promise."

Luke nodded too before holding out his hand to Emiliea. She glanced up at him nervously before taking his hand as they both made their way into the cave. The change was immediate. The air inside seemed heavier and wetter causing both of them to begin sweating even more profusely. The odd thing was, the cave walls were completely dry. Although the air was humid and wet, not a single stone had a single drop of moisture on it.

"This is so weird," Luke commented looking around.

"I know. Let's just find what we need and go," Emiliea replied, her heart rate speeding up as they made their way deeper in the cave. She continued walking until she came to a hole in the floor. However, in the darkness she did not see it and instead went tumbling down screaming, Luke following.

"Are you ok?" she asked when they landed at the bottom. When there was no response, she began to panic. She turned around to see Luke staring at something. Following his gaze she saw the unmistakable sight of an ancient Old World city.

"This must be it," Luke said in awe. "The fallen city."

Emiliea nodded as she stood up dusting off her clothing. They continued forward into the city on guard. The place reeked of death. Skeletons lay strewn about on the floor as they made their way further into the city. They came across a large building in the center of the city. The surrounding area was littered with bones and rubble. It appeared to be a temple of some kind. They entered cautiously, not wanting to disturb the site.

"Look at that," Emiliea said pointing to the skeleton in the center of the mass. The dead man was holding a scroll in a death grip. Carefully, she walked up to him and pried the scroll out of his hands. "This is it," She yelled in triumph. "This is the cure. We have to get this to Eliza."

The pair sprinted out of the city

as quickly as they could and found Eliza and Cora waiting for them back by the plane.

"We got it," Luke said. "This is it, right?" he asked Eliza, handing her the scroll. She looked over it quickly and nodded.

"We found it," She said happily. "We actually found it."

"Well what are we waiting for?" Cora asked jubilantly. "We have to get this back to the Center doctors."

"Let's go," Emiliea nodded. They were back in the sky within minutes, racing through the air to their final destination.

Again Emiliea found herself in the copilot's seat. Luke noticed her as she entered and put the plane on autopilot before turning to talk to her.

"What's up?"

"I just wanted to thank you," Emiliea said. "For everything. I have a chance to save my brother now."

"Emi this was all you. None of this would have happened without you. You are without a doubt the most badass woman I know. And you're a good person. The bravest one I've ever met," he replied honestly.

"Thank you," She said blushing. She turned towards him gazing deeply into his eyes. "You really think I'm brave?"

"Of course you are," Luke responded.

Emiliea nodded taking all of this in. She took a deep breath before leaning forward and kissing him.

"Yeah I guess I am," she agreed, smiling. Luke smiled back and put an arm over her shoulder.

"I'm glad you're in my life Emi," He said happily.

"Me too."

They touched down in Siberia a few hours later and were greeted with fifteen armed guards.

"Don't shoot," Emiliea said, hopping out of the plane. "We need to speak with the medics at the Center. We found a cure."

They were led in quickly and Eliza followed the guards to the doctor. However, the rest of them were forced to wait outside as they had no medical experience and were unable to translate the cure. Angela found them a few minutes later, racing over to drag her daughter into a huge embrace.

"You're alive," she said tearfully, clinging tightly to Emiliea. "I can't believe you're alive."

"I told you I'd come back,"

Emiliea replied tearfully. "Is Kevin ok?"

Angela looked at her daughter sadly and shook her head.

"He progressed into stage three last night," she rasped. "He won't make it through the night." Emiliea felt tears streaming down her cheeks at the statement.

"Can I see him please?"

Angela looked at her daughter biting her lip nervously before nodding.

"Come with me."

As Emiliea was led down the sterile white corridors, the rest of the world seemed to fade out of existence. Her mother stopped outside the door and gestured to it, allowing Emiliea to enter alone. The sight before her was awful. Kevin had always been a pale child, but in this instance, he was whiter than the sheets of his bed. His shaky breaths were the only way you could have seen he was still alive, and his nose continued to bleed.

"Hey Kevin," Emiliea said gently, walking forward towards him. "How are you feeling?"

The only response was the echo of silence stinging her ears.

"I found it," Emiliea continued. "Kev, I found the cure. I just need you to hold on a little longer, ok? Please." She grasped his hand in hers and squeezed tightly hoping to get some sort of response, but there was nothing. He didn't even move his head. "Please just, stay with me a little longer ok? I can't lose you Kevin." More tears began to fall from her eyes. She didn't know what to do. She'd found the cure so it had to be ok. He had to live, it wasn't fair otherwise.

"I need you," she whispered hoarsely. "Don't do this to me. I'm nothing without you."

A small pressure was placed on her hand as she looked up at her brother's face. His hazel eyes met her wet violet ones as blood began to trickle from his mouth. He stared at her longingly before taking another shuddering breath. The pressure on her hand disappeared as the life drained out of his eyes. His chest stopped moving and the silence that descended was unbearable. The room suffocated her as she moved over her brother's lifeless body and put her hand on his cold face. Moving her hands, Emiliea watched as she closed her brother's eyes forever. She was too late. They were all too late. A tight feeling constricted over her chest as she clung to her brother's corpse rocking back and forth with him held closely in her arms. She wiped the blood off his mouth and released a guttural scream.

ABOUT THE AUTHOR

Zophia Kotala is a Florida high school student who wrote Scorching Siberian Winter. She is striving to write fictional stories that communicate real world issues Gen Z faces currently or will have to face in the future. Her first work is a Scorching Siberian Winter. While it originally started as just another school project, it quickly turned into something she was passionate about. It was the perfect way to raise her voice and bring issues society faces to light. She has loved writing ever since she was a young girl often using it as a creative escape into entirely new worlds, but being able to write a story that was fun to write while also sharing concerns about the future made her realize that this was something she would continue to do long past a due date.